Decorating Sabir's Room

Written by
Maggie Freeman

Illustrated by
Helen Stanton

Ransom

"It's time to decorate your room," Mum says. "What colour do you want it?"

Sabir looks at the colour chart. "Orange is my favourite colour," he says.

But Dad says, "That orange is too bright. Let's get this pale one."

Sabir measures his room to find out how much paint they need. He holds one end of the tape and Dad holds the other.

Each wall is 3 metres long. Sabir multiplies by 4 to find his room is 12 metres around.

He measures the height of the room. It is more than 2 metres high. "Now I know how much paint we need," says Dad.

Sabir and Dad drive to the shop and find the paint they need – pale orange paint for the walls and white for the ceiling; and a small tin of white gloss for the woodwork.

They put all the tins in the trolley, Dad pays, and they both drive home.

Sabir has to take all the things out of his room. He puts his jigsaws and LEGO and football in a cardboard box. He puts his books and drawings in another box. He puts all his clothes in a suitcase. Dad takes out Sabir's shelves and puts everything in his and Mum's room.

On Saturday morning Sabir wakes up when Mum shakes him. "Come on, sleepy head," she says. "Time to start work."

Sabir gets up. Mum and Dad carry his bed into his sisters' room. Sabir goes back to bed again. One of Sabir's sisters throws soft toys down on him from the top bunk, so he gets up again.

Sabir finds Dad in his room, putting up the stepladder. "Catch!" Dad shouts. He throws the curtains down, and Sabir catches them. Then together Sabir and Dad spread a plastic sheet over the floor, to protect it from paint splashes.

Then Dad uses sandpaper to rub the skirting boards – the wooden boards around the bottom of the walls. "What are you doing that for, Dad?" Sabir asks.

"So the new paint will stay on better," says Dad.

Sabir gets water, a bucket and a sponge, and washes the skirting boards. Dad climbs up the stepladder again. "Pass me the roller, please," he says, "then I can paint the ceiling."

When the skirting boards are dry, Sabir paints them with a brush. It doesn't matter if he gets a bit of paint on the walls. "Well done!" Dad says to Sabir. "You've done a really good job."

When Sabir wakes up the next morning, Dad is already up the stepladder. He is painting the walls of Sabir's room. Sabir stands and watches. He wishes the walls were a bright orange colour.

Mum comes and watches too. Sabir says, "My friend Max has stickers on his walls."

"You can order some if you like," Mum says.

She opens her laptop and Sabir scans lots of pictures of wall stickers. "I like that rocket," he says, "and that alien. And stars to go on my ceiling, please, Mum."

At last Dad finishes painting the walls. He stands back in the doorway and says, "There. That looks good. I hope you're happy with it too."

"Will you help me wash the rollers and brushes, so we can use them another time?" Dad says. Sabir helps his dad.

Mum takes the stepladder downstairs, and folds up the plastic sheet. Sabir's room feels cold and bare and smells of fresh paint.

"We have to let the paint dry properly," Mum says. "You'll have to sleep in your sisters' room for a few days."

The following Saturday, Sabir carries his duvet and pillow back in to his room. Mum and Dad carry his bed back in.

Sabir and Dad carry his shelves back in to his room. Sabir puts the bolts back in and Dad tightens them with a screwdriver. Sabir fills his shelves with his toys and clothes.

Mum hangs his curtains up again. "We have to wait 30 days to put the stickers on the walls," Mum says. "It says so in the instructions."

Thirty days later, Sabir's room is finished. His rocket sticker is huge and the alien is smiley. Sabir lies in his comfy bed, looking up at the shiny star stickers on the ceiling.

Sabir is very happy with his new room.